EMERSON BARKS

Liza Woodruff

Christy Ottaviano Books
Henry Holt and Company
NEW YORK

For Tom

Henry Holt and Company, LLC
Publishers since 1866
175 Fifth Avenue
New York, New York 10010
mackids.com

Library of Congress Cataloging-in-Publication Data
Woodruff, Liza, author, illustrator.
Emerson barks / Liza Woodruff.—First edition.
pages   cm
Summary: "A little dog with a big bark saves the day"–Provided by publisher.
ISBN 978-1-62779-167-0 (hardback)
[1. Dogs–Fiction. 2. Behavior–Fiction.] I. Title.
PZ7.W8615Em 2016   [E]–dc23   2015015548

Our books may be purchased in bulk for promotional, educational, or business use.
Please contact your local bookseller or the Macmillan Corporate and Premium Sales Department
at (800) 221-7945 ext. 5442 or by e-mail at MacmillanSpecialMarkets@macmillan.com.

First Edition—2016 / Designed by Anna Booth
The illustrations were created with pen and ink, and with digital pen, paint, and pastel using Adobe Photoshop.
Printed in China by Toppan Leefung Printing Ltd., Dongguan City, Guangdong Province

10 9 8 7 6 5 4 3 2 1

Emerson was a tiny little dog. But he had a great big . . .

Life was great for Emerson.

He loved his girl, Eva,
and she loved him.

He liked to visit his neighbor Miss Cross and her cat, Kissy, and they always enjoyed seeing him.
(Well, sort of.)

One day, things changed for Emerson.

K!

It was a lovely morning and Emerson couldn't wait to greet his friends.

But as Emerson said hello,
Kissy said good-bye.

Kissy disappeared, and that afternoon, while Emerson searched the area . . .

Miss Cross paid Eva a visit.
"That big-mouthed dog of yours made
Kissy run away!" she sputtered.

"Emerson,
that's it!"

NO MORE BARKING!

Emerson could see that Eva
was upset. He went to his bed
and curled up in a little ball.

Later, when Emerson felt excitement stirring in his throat, he caught himself just in time. "*AR-ahem*," he coughed.

When the mail came,
Emerson gulped to keep
in another bark.

After finishing his business at the end
of the day, he swallowed two more barks
and felt his collar tighten a little.

That night, Emerson's tummy hurt.

He tossed
and turned,

but he couldn't
get comfortable.

Too many barks inside, he thought.

The next morning,
Emerson found it very
difficult to stay quiet.

He paced

and chewed,

but pacing and chewing didn't make his collar feel looser or stop his stomach and head from hurting. There was only one thing that *would* make him feel better.

Emerson followed his nose.

He tried

and tried

and tried to get
someone's attention.

 Now, even more than before, his head ached, his tummy hurt, and his collar pinched.

 A strange feeling prickled his paws.

It crept through his tummy and into his throat.

He swallowed hard.

Just then, something stirred in the bushes. Before he could stop himself, Emerson opened his mouth.

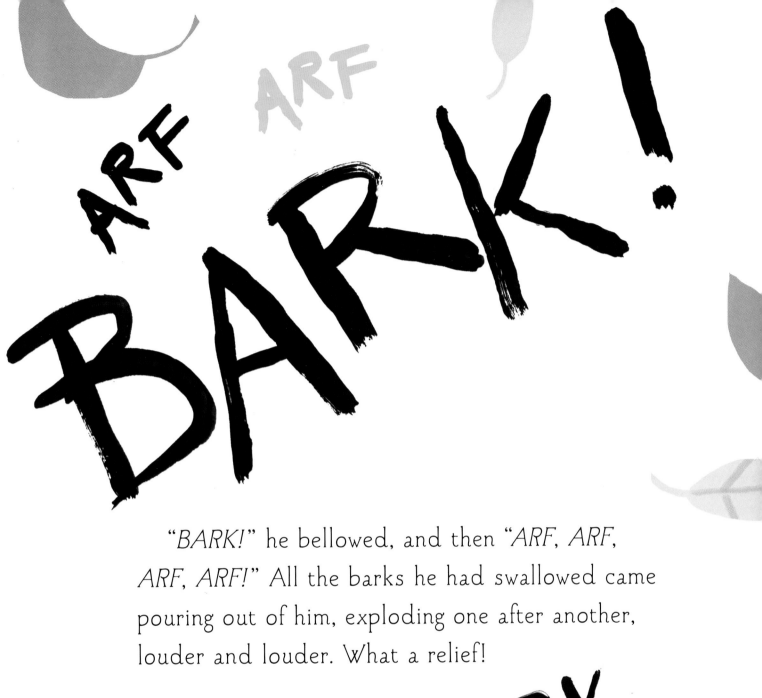

"*BARK!*" he bellowed, and then "*ARF, ARF, ARF, ARF!*" All the barks he had swallowed came pouring out of him, exploding one after another, louder and louder. What a relief!

Eva came running,

Miss Cross came running,

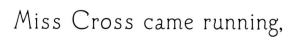

and the postman paused.

Emerson had found Kissy!

But she was not alone.

"GOOD BOY!"
shouted Eva.

"SMART DOG!"
praised the postman.

"MY HERO!"
gushed Miss Cross.

Things quickly returned to
normal in the neighborhood. . . .

Well, almost.